# Ben

This Book Belongs
To: Miss Jodi
   Chamberlin

a mary bee creation

# Ben

Ben is one in a series of Predictable Reading Books written by Mary Buckman. Books in this series are designed to help children read naturally and easily as they become involved in the repetitive rhythmic pattern of the language.

by
Mary
Buckman

Illustrated by Connie Morgan

**Library of Congress Catalog Card Number: 90-093586**

**ISBN 1-879414-09-0**

For the parents and staff of
San Mateo Park School, a team *dedicated* to
meeting the special needs of ALL children.

Ben Spangenberg, a spina bifida child, lives in California with his family and his cat "Pudding-Face." He loves chocolate ice cream, swimming, and babies, but his favorite thing is his "Will Clark" bat.

He knows all the planets in the solar system and if he does not grow up to be an orthopedic surgeon or a writer, he plans to be an astronomer.

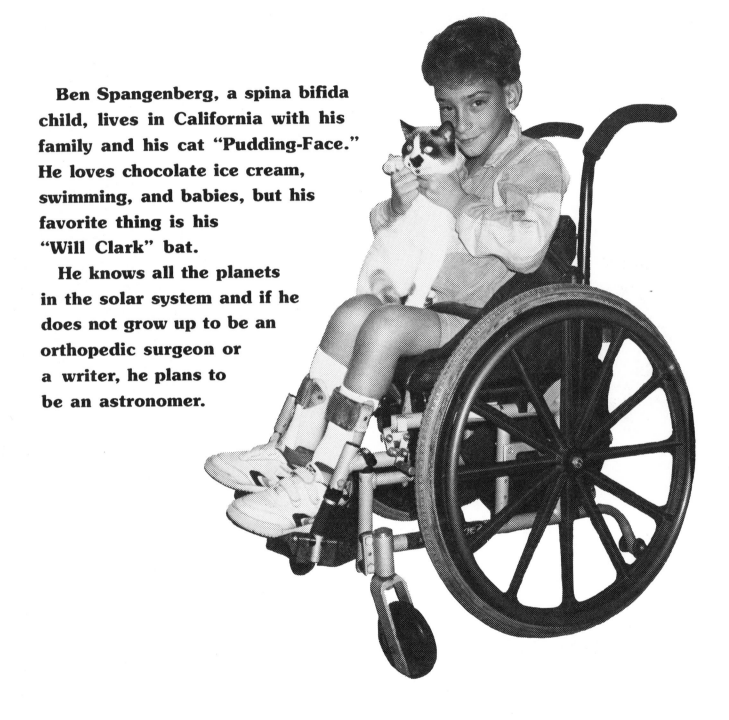

**The first day of school**
   **I was nervous and shy**
**I felt like hiding**
   **When a voice said,**

"HI . . . This is Scotty,
and Eva and Jen.
I'm pleased to meet you!
My name's BEN!"

**Our teacher said, "Salute,"
And we all stood tall,
Respectful of the flag
On the classroom wall.**

**With hand over heart
To say, "I care,"
Ben straightened up
In his WHEELCHAIR!**

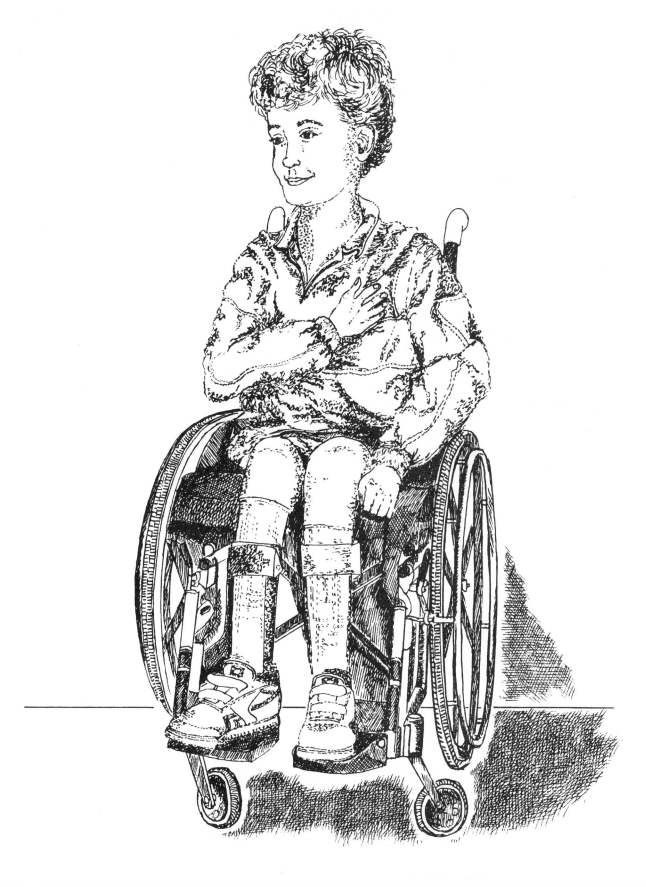

**Our class had P.E.**
     **On the playground lawn,**
**Sliding into bases**
     **Where the grass was gone.**

**Just to be sure**
**That the game was fair,**
**Ben played umpire**
**In his WHEELCHAIR!**

**The Halloween Parade**
      **Brought excitement to school,**
**With prizes for the best-dressed**
      **Goblin and ghoul.**

**But first prize went**
**To a big brown bear**
**Bumping along**
**In a WHEELCHAIR!**

**In Computer Lab,
We started to write
The stories we drafted
For homework last night.**

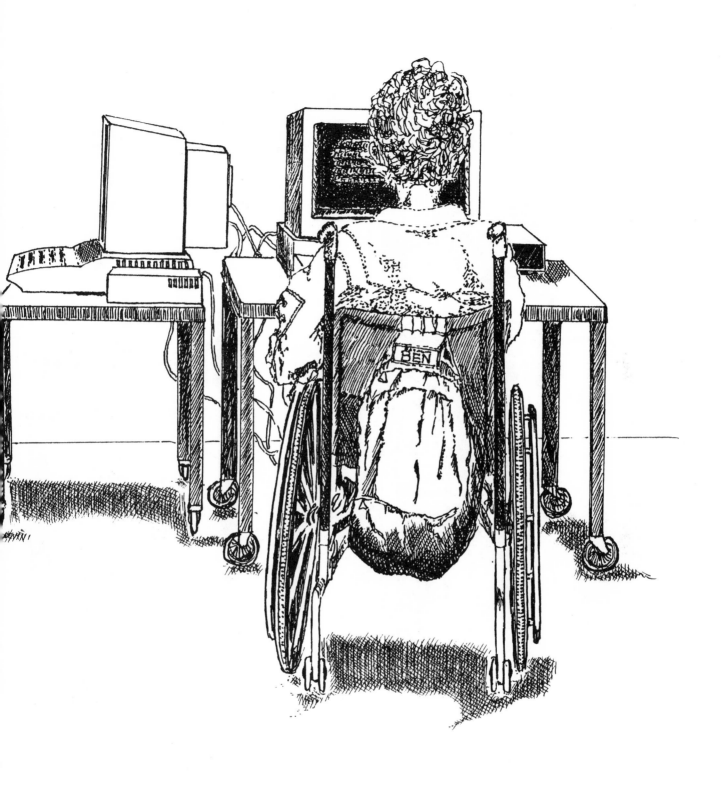

**With screen tilted down
To lessen the glare,
Ben worked the keyboard
In his WHEELCHAIR!**

**Our class was deep in study
Of how the West was won.
The teacher said we'd give reports,
And that it would be fun!**

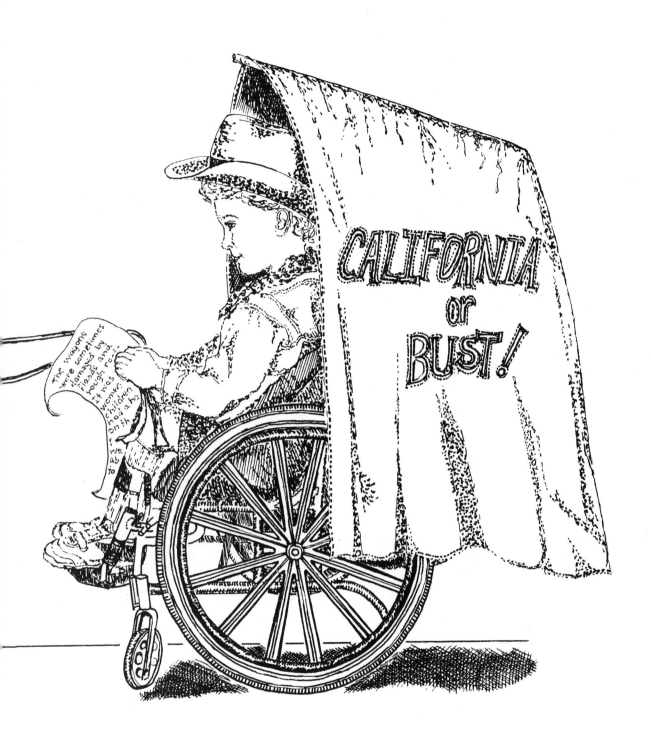

**So I was the reporter,
   Megan was the mare,
And Ben summed up our findings
   In a covered WHEELCHAIR!**

**The school talent show
Was Saturday night
With friends doing skits
In a bright spotlight.**

**There were poems and songs**
**And dancing to share,**
**And Ben performed "WHEELIES"**
**In his WHEELCHAIR!**

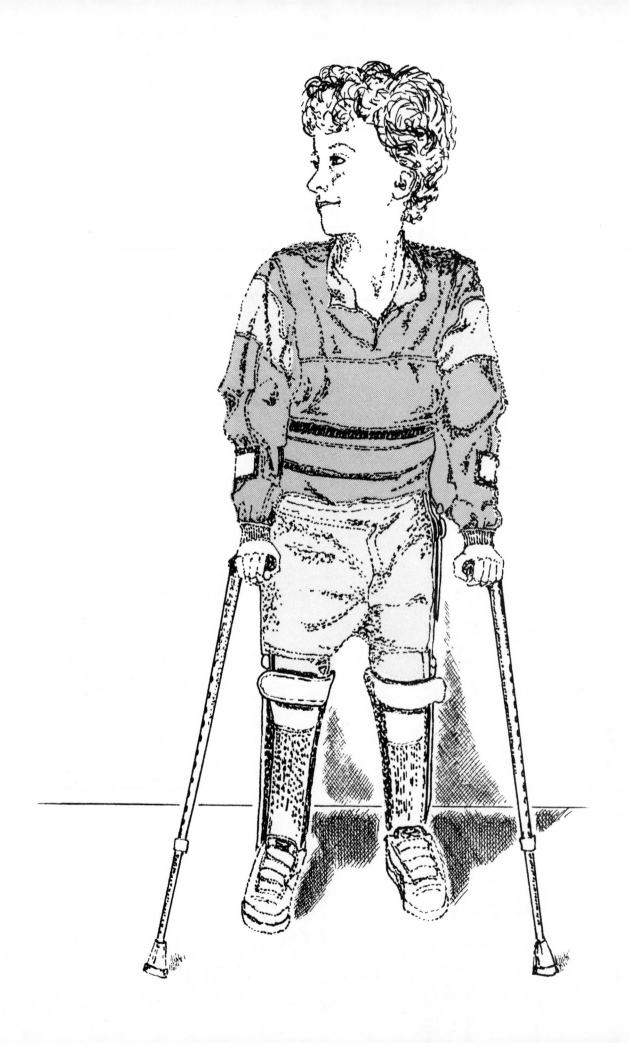

I've learned from Ben that if you have
   A dream within your heart,
Your dream can't be reality
   Till you stand up and start!

It doesn't matter HOW you start:
   Slowly, or with pep...
The most important thing is that you
   TAKE THE FIRST STEP!


And if at first you don't succeed,
   Then try, and try AGAIN!
NOW I  know what these things mean
   'Cause I've spent time with BEN!

**"BEN IS SPECIAL."**
**This is what I heard my teacher say.**
**I know what she means**
**Because I think it every day.**

**With head upon my pillow
As day comes to an end, I think...**

THAT
SPECIAL
GUY IS...

MY
BEST
FRIEND!

Typesetting and computer design
by
**Susan Alvaro**
PO Box 905
El Granada, CA  94018